About Wise Men and Simpletons

TWELVE TALES FROM GRIMM

About Wise Men and Simpletons

TWELVE TALES FROM GRIMM, *Jakob*

TRANSLATED BY ELIZABETH SHUB

ETCHINGS BY NONNY HOGROGIAN

The Macmillan Company, New York · Collier-Macmillan Ltd., London

The etchings have been reproduced in halftone. The typeface is English Monotype Bembo.

Contents

Foreword

All the stories in this collection, with the exception of "The Bremen Town Musicians," were translated from the *Kinder- Und Hausmärchen* ("Children's and Household Stories") by Jacob and Wilhelm Grimm as originally published. The first volume appeared in 1812, the second in 1815. "The Bremen Town Musicians" was not included until a later edition. The work began as a scholarly project: the systematic recording for ethnological purposes of German folklore. Like other folk literature, these stories had existed mainly in the precarious safekeeping of memory, handed down by word of mouth from generation to generation. Now for the first time the tales and legends were written down in the straightforward style and language of the people, just as they had been told, many of them in their local dialects.

Although the first volume of the *Kinder- Und Hausmärchen* was received rather coldly by the press, it was an immediate success with the reading public, and when the second volume appeared it had a ready audience. The work of gathering material did not stop and in 1819 the brothers published an enlarged and revised edition. Through five successive editions, the last of which appeared in 1857, they continued to make changes and "improve" the collection.

As time went on, different versions of stories came to their attention. There were variations and additions depending on the district of origin of the individual storyteller, and even on the later recollections of forgotten incidents by the original tellers. But the addition or deletion of a detail, verse, or incident did not make one Grimm version more authentic than another, nor was it a matter of better or worse. It was a reflection of the Grimms' thorough, scientific approach. The fact that the *Kinder- Und Hausmärchen* turned out to be a masterpiece as well is one of the most fortunate of literary accidents.

A selection of twelve stories from the over two hundred collected by the Brothers Grimm must obviously be a personal one. Nonny Hogrogian and I first thought that we would like to do a book of the lesser-known tales. But when the final choice had to be made, it became clear that the ones we liked best were in most instances among the most famous of the stories. They required no adaptation and could be rendered into English with as little deviation from the original as a viable translation would allow.

I chose also to translate the first Grimm edition because I felt that many of its versions have a conciseness that is in tune with the modern reader. Though incidents added in later editions are often charming in themselves (such as the duck that takes Hansel and

Gretel across the lake on their way home from the witch's house), they are in no sense intrinsic to the story. And if some of the endings in the stories translated here seem a bit precipitous, and not the rounded summations adapters of fairy tales have got us into the habit of expecting, a second reading will show that the story ended because there really was nothing more to tell.

The total unselfconsciousness of the stories in the initial edition endows them with the special power of a spoken story. Here, even more than in the later editions, the storyteller's voice is omnipresent. The nuance of a pause, the connotation of an inflection are inevitably conveyed. The self-confidence and honesty of the telling make unimportant the occasional disregard for such sophisticated requirements of modern writing as consistency, credibility, time element.

In the words of the Grimms themselves: "We do not need to praise or defend these stories. They are protected by the very fact of their existence."

New York, 1971   *Elizabeth Shub*

About Wise Men and Simpletons

TWELVE TALES FROM GRIMM

About a Fisherman and His Wife

About a Fisherman and His Wife

Once there was a fisherman, who lived with his wife in a hovel close by the sea. Each day he went down to the water and fished, and so it had been going on for a long time.

One day as he sat fishing and gazing into the clear water, watching his line, it suddenly sank deep under. When he reeled it up, there was a big flounder at the end of it. The flounder said to him, "I bid you let me live, for I am not really a flounder, but an enchanted prince. Set me back into the water and let me swim away."

"Well," said the fisherman, "no need for so many words. Any flounder that talks, I'm glad to let swim."

Then he set the flounder back into the water and the flounder swam straight down to the ocean bed, leaving a red streak of blood behind him.

The man went home to his wife and told her that he had caught a flounder that said it was an enchanted prince and so he had put it back into the water.

"And you didn't wish for anything?" said his wife.

"No," said the fisherman. "What should I have wished for?"

"Oh," said his wife, "it's so nasty to have to live in this pig sty forever. It's smelly and dirty. Go back and wish us a nice little cottage."

It didn't seem quite right to the fisherman, but nevertheless he went to the sea, and when he got there, he saw that the water had turned all yellow and green. He walked to the water's edge and said:

> "*Mandje! Mandje! Timpe Te!*
> *Flounder, flounder, in the sea!*
> *My wife, whose name is Ilsebill,*
> *Will not have things as I will.*"

The flounder came swimming up and said, "Well, then, what does she want?"

"Oh," said the fisherman, "my wife says since I caught you, I should have wished for something. She doesn't want to live in a pig sty any longer. She wants a little cottage."

"Go home," said the flounder, "and you'll find her in it."

So the man went home and there was his wife standing in the doorway of a cottage. "Come on in," she said. "Now, isn't this much better?" Inside there was a large room and a smaller room, and behind the house, there was a little garden with all kinds of vegetables growing in it, and a yard where there were chickens and ducks.

"Oh," said the man, "now we can live here and be content."

"Yes," said the wife, "we will try."

And so everything went well for a week or two, and then the wife said, "Husband! There's not enough room in this cottage. The yard and garden are too small. I want to live in a big stone castle. Go to the flounder and tell him to give us a castle."

"But, Wife," said the fisherman, "the flounder has just given us this cottage. I don't like the idea of going to him again. He may get annoyed."

"Well, I want it," said the wife. "He can do it, and he'll do it willingly. Go on, now."

The fisherman went to the sea, but his heart was heavy. The water had turned violet and gray and dark blue, though it was still calm. He stood at the water's edge and said:

> *"Mandje! Mandje! Timpe Te!*
> *Flounder, flounder, in the sea!*
> *My wife, whose name is Ilsebill,*
> *Will not have things as I will."*

"Well, then, what does she want?" said the flounder.

"Oh," said the man quite unhappily, "my wife wants a stone castle to live in."

"Go home, and you'll find her standing in front of the door," said the flounder.

The man went home and there stood his wife in front of a great castle.

"Look, Husband," she said, "isn't it beautiful?" And they went in together. There were many servants. The walls were smooth, and the main hall was furnished with benches and tables of gold. Behind the castle there was a garden, and a park, about a half a mile long, in which there were stags and does and rabbits. And in the courtyard stood a barn for cows and a stable for horses.

"Oh," said the man, "we will remain in this beautiful palace and be contented."

"We'll think about that," said his wife. "We'll sleep on it." And they went to bed.

The following morning the wife awoke at dawn. She poked her husband in the side with her elbow and said, "Husband, get up. We want to be king over all this land."

"Oh, Wife," said the husband, "why should we be king? I don't want to be king."

"Well then, I'll be king."

"Oh, Wife," said the man, "king of what? The flounder can't do that."

"Husband," said the wife, "go, at once. I want to be king."

And so the man went to the sea, but was most unhappy that his wife wanted to be king. As he came to the water, he saw that it was black-gray, with the waves swirling up from below. He stood at the water's edge and said:

"*Mandje! Mandje! Timpe Te!*
Flounder, flounder, in the sea!
My wife, whose name is Ilsebill,
Will not have things as I will."

"Well, what does she want?" said the flounder.

"Oh," said the fisherman, "my wife wants to be king."

"Go home. She is," said the flounder.

So the fisherman went home and saw a palace surrounded by many soldiers. There were drummers and trumpeters, and his wife sat within, on a tall throne of gold and diamonds. She wore a large crown of gold, and on either side of her, stood a row of sweet ladies-in-waiting, each a head shorter than the one behind her.

"Now then," said the man, "are you king?"

"Yes," she said, "I am king."

After gazing at her for a while the fisherman said, "Well, Wife, now will you let it be? You're king, and we don't need to wish for anything more."

"No, Husband," she said, "time hangs heavily on my hands. I can't stand it any more. I am king, but now I want to be emperor."

"But, Wife," said the husband, "he can't make you emperor. I can't ask the flounder for that."

"I am king," said the wife, "and you're only my husband. Go, at once."

The fisherman left, and as he walked along, he thought to himself, "It's no good. It's got out of hand. To want to be emperor is shameless. The flounder will lose his patience."

With that he came to the sea which had turned black and murky, and such a sharp wind swept over it that it churned the water. He stood at the water's edge and said:

"Mandje! Mandje! Timpe Te!
Flounder, flounder, in the sea!
My wife, whose name is Ilsebill,
Will not have things as I will."

"Well, what does she want?" said the flounder.

"Oh," said the fisherman, "my wife wants to be emperor."

"Go home," said the flounder. "She is."

The fisherman went home and when he got there, he found his wife sitting on a very high throne. It was made of solid gold, and she wore a great crown some six feet high. On either side of her stood her gentlemen-at-arms, each one shorter than the one behind him. They ranged in size from the tallest guards down to the smallest dwarfs—as tiny as one's little finger. Before her stood a crowd of counts and barons. The fisherman came to her and said, "Wife, are you emperor?"

"Yes," she said. "I am emperor."

"Wife," said the fisherman, looking her squarely in the eye, "now that you're emperor, that's enough!"

"Husband," said she, "why do you stand there? I am emperor, but I want to be Pope."

"Oh, Wife," said the fisherman, "why do you want to be Pope? There is only one pope in Christendom."

"Husband," said she, "I want to be Pope before the day is out."

"No, Wife," said he, "the flounder can't make you Pope. This won't end well."

"Husband, what nonsense! If he can make an emperor, he can make a pope. Go, at once."

The fisherman decided to go, but felt faint. His hands and legs shook. Outside the wind raged, the ocean seethed. The ships, tossed about on the waves, signaled in distress. In the middle of the sky there was still a patch of blue, but in the south the sky had turned red with the gathering thunderstorm.

The fisherman stood at the water's edge, and in despair, he said:

"Mandje! Mandje! Timpe Te!
Flounder, flounder, in the sea!
My wife, whose name is Ilsebill,
Will not have things as I will."

"Now what does she want?" said the flounder.

"Oh," said the fisherman, "my wife wants to be Pope."

"Go home," said the flounder. "She is."

So he went home and when he got there he saw his wife sitting on a throne two miles high. She wore three huge crowns, and was surrounded by men of priestly state. On either side of her stood a row of candles, the tallest as thick as a tower, the smallest a thin taper.

"Wife," said the fisherman, looking straight at her, "are you now Pope?"

"Yes," she said, "I am Pope."

"Well," said the fisherman, "now that you are Pope, let it be. Wife, you must be satisfied, for Pope is the most that you can be."

"I'll think about it," said the wife, and they went to bed. But she was not contented and her greed would not let her sleep. She kept thinking what else she might want to be, until the sun rose. "Ha," she thought, as she looked out of the window and saw the sun. "Why can't I make the sun come up?" She poked her husband and said grimly, "Husband, go to the flounder. I want to be as the dear Lord is."

The fisherman, who was still half asleep, was so frightened that he fell out of bed.

"Wife," he said, "leave well enough alone and remain Pope."

"No," said his wife, "I'm not satisfied. I can't stand it when I see the sun and the moon rise and know that I can't make them do it. I want to be as the dear Lord is."

"But, Wife," said the fisherman, "the flounder can't do that. He can make an emperor and a pope, but he can't do that."

"Husband," said she, "I want to be as the dear Lord is. Go at once to the flounder." And she gave him such a wild look that the fisherman trembled with fear.

Outside the storm raged, bending trees and toppling boulders. The sky was black, and it thundered and lightened, and the dark waves of the sea rose into mountains crowned with white foam. The fisherman stood there and said:

> "*Mandje! Mandje! Timpe Te!*
> *Flounder, flounder, in the sea!*
> *My wife, whose name is Ilsebill,*
> *Will not have things as I will.*"

"Now what does she want?" said the flounder.

"Alas," said the fisherman, "she wants to be as the dear Lord is."

"Go home. You'll find her back in her pig sty."

And there they are to this day.

The Wolf and the Seven Kids

The Wolf and the Seven Kids

A goat had seven kids whom she loved dearly and guarded carefully against the wolf. One day when she had to go out for provisions, she called them all together and said, "Dear children, I must go and bring food. Beware of the wolf and don't let him in. Listen carefully, because he often tries to disguise himself. You will always be able to recognize him by his hoarse voice and black paws. Be watchful, for once he gets into the house, he'll eat you all up."

Then she left and, before long, the wolf stood at the door and called, "Dear children, open up, I'm your mother and I've brought back some lovely things for you."

But the seven kids replied, "You are not our mother. She has a soft, pleasing voice, and your voice is hoarse. You are the wolf and we won't let you in."

The wolf went to a storekeeper from whom he bought a large piece of chalk. He ate the chalk and it made his voice sound soft. He returned to the house of the seven kids and spoke gently, "Dear

17

children, let me in. I am your mother and I have something for each of you."

But he had set his paws on the windowsill, and the seven kids saw them and said, "You are not our mother. None of her feet is black like yours. You are the wolf and we won't let you in."

The wolf went to a baker and said, "Cover my paws with freshly made dough." When the baker had done so, the wolf went to the miller and said, "Sprinkle white flour over my paws." The miller refused. "If you don't do it, I'll eat you up," said the wolf, and the miller was forced to do what the wolf asked. When the miller had finished, the wolf went back to the house of the seven kids. He stood by the door and said, "Dear children, let me in. I am your mother and I have a present for each of you."

The seven kids first asked to see the wolf's paws, and when they saw that they were snow-white and heard how softly he spoke, they thought he was their mother and opened the door. The wolf came in. As soon as they recognized him, they hid quickly, as best they could. The first got under the table, the second into the bed, the third into the oven, the fourth ran into the kitchen, the fifth hid in the cupboard, the sixth slid under a big pot, and the seventh squeezed himself into the grandfather clock. But the wolf found all of them and swallowed them whole, except the youngest, hidden in the clock. He was saved.

Since the wolf had satisfied his appetite, he left and soon afterward the goat returned home. What a hue and cry! The wolf had been there and had eaten her children! She thought they were all gone until the youngest jumped out of the clock, and related how the tragedy had taken place.

In the meantime, the wolf, because he had eaten so much, took himself off to a green meadow, lay down in the sunlight and fell fast asleep.

The old goat thought that, somehow, she might still save her children, and so she said to the youngest kid, "Take some yarn, a needle and a pair of shears, and follow me."

She went out in search of the wolf and found him snoring in the meadow. "Here he lies, the horrid wolf, after having eaten my six children for an afternoon snack," she said, as she inspected him carefully from all sides. "Let me have the shears. If only they are still alive inside him."

Then she cut open his stomach and the six kids, which in his greed the wolf had swallowed whole, sprang out unharmed. The goat told them to go at once and find some heavy stones. Then they filled the wolf's stomach with the stones, sewed him up and hid themselves behind some brushwood.

When the wolf had had his sleep, he awoke, but he felt so heavy that he said, "All this rumbling and grumbling inside me, what can it be? I only ate six kids."

He thought perhaps a drink of fresh water would help him and went off to the spring. But when he bent down to drink, he lost his balance because of the heavy stones within him and plunged headlong into the water. The seven kids, who had been watching, came running from their hiding place and danced around the spring for joy.

Brier Rose

Brier Rose

A king and queen, who had no child, wanted nothing more than to have one.

One day as the queen was bathing in a lake, a crab crawled out of the water onto the shore and said, "Your wish is to come true, for soon you will bear a daughter."

And so it happened. The king was overjoyed at the birth of a princess and ordered a great feast prepared. Among the guests invited were the famous dowager fairies of the land. But as the king had only twelve golden plates and there were thirteen of these ladies, one had to be left out. The invited fairies all came, and at the end of the banquet, each stepped forward to present the child with a gift. The first endowed her with virtue, the second gave her beauty, until each in turn had bestowed on the little princess all the worldly blessings anyone could wish for.

But just as the eleventh fairy had announced her gift, the thirteenth, furious that she had not been invited, appeared in the hall and cried out, "Because I was not asked to come here, I say that when your daughter is fifteen, she will prick herself on a spindle and fall dead."

The parents were terrified at these words, but the twelfth fairy, who had not yet spoken, said, "No, she will not die. Instead she will fall into a deep sleep that will last for a hundred years."

The king, who hoped somehow to save his beloved child, ordered all the spindles in the kingdom destroyed. The princess grew up and became a miracle of beauty. One day soon after her fifteenth birthday, the king and queen went visiting and the princess remained behind in the palace. She wandered about the grounds at will and finally came upon an ancient tower with a narrow stairway leading up to it. She was curious, and followed the stairs to the top where there was a little door with a key in its lock. She turned the key and the door sprang open, revealing a small room where an old woman sat spinning flax. She liked the old woman on sight and soon asked her if she might not try some spinning herself. As she spoke, she teasingly reached for the spindle and had barely touched it when it pricked her. She fell down and was at once in a deep sleep.

The king and queen, and their retinue, had at that moment returned to the palace, and the whole court began to fall asleep: the horses in the stables, the doves on the roof, the mottled hunting dogs in the courtyard, the flies on the walls—even the fire in the hearth flickered and went out. The roast stopped sputtering; the cook, who was about to pull the hair of the kitchen boy, let him go; and the maid dropped the hen she was plucking. A thick hedge of thorn and

25859

bramble sprang up around the castle. It rose higher and higher until the castle was completely hidden from view.

Many princes heard about beautiful Brier Rose and came to the sleeping court hoping to break the spell that held it. But not one of them was able to force his way through the thick hedge that surrounded the castle. They became imprisoned in the clawlike brambles. Once in their grasp, the princes were unable to free themselves and remained there, moaning until they died.

In this way many years went by, until it happened that a prince who was traveling through the land heard from an old man that, behind a thick bramble hedge, there stood a castle where, it was believed, a wonderfully beautiful princess and her entire court slept and could not be awakened. The old man's grandfather had told him about the many princes who had tried to break through the hedge and that not one of them had escaped death among the piercing thorns and brambles.

"That does not frighten me," said the prince. "I will force my way through and free Brier Rose." He made his way to the place where the tall hedge stood, and when he came close to it, he found not brambles, but blossoms that separated to let him pass, but which immediately turned to thorns again behind him. He soon reached the castle and found the horses and mottled hunting dogs asleep in the courtyard. On the roof the doves sat with their heads tucked beneath their wings. The prince entered the castle and saw the flies asleep on the walls, the hearth cold, the cook and maid asleep in the kitchen. He continued on through the entire silent household, and finally he came to the sleeping king and queen. It was so still that he could hear his own breathing.

At last he entered the ancient tower in which Brier Rose lay sleeping. The prince was so awed by her beauty, that he knelt down and kissed her. She awoke at once, as did the king and queen and the entire court. The horses and the dogs awoke, the doves moved on the roof and the flies on the walls. In the kitchen the fire rekindled itself and continued cooking the roast, which sputtered on. The cook got up and boxed the kitchen boy's ear and the maid finished plucking the hen. The wedding of Brier Rose and the prince was celebrated that day and they lived contentedly together for the rest of their lives.

About Elves

About Elves

THE ELVES AND THE SHOEMAKER WHOSE WORK THEY DID

A shoemaker had grown so poor that he had only enough leather left to make one pair of shoes. In the evening he cut them out so that he would be ready to start work first thing in the morning. Then he went to bed, but when he awoke next day and sat down at his work bench, he found a pair of shoes, all finished and beautifully made. Soon a customer came in and paid so well for the shoes that the shoemaker was able to buy enough leather to make two new pairs. These he also cut out in the evening, and again in the morning when he sat down to work there they were, two pairs, perfectly made. And for the money he received when he sold them, the shoemaker was able to buy leather for four pairs. On the third morning, too, the shoes stood already finished on his table. And so it continued. As many shoes as the shoemaker cut out at night, so many stood ready the following morning. And soon he was well-to-do again.

One night, shortly before Christmas, as the shoemaker was

about to go to bed, he said to his wife, "Shouldn't we stay up just once and see who has been doing our work for us?"

And so they lit a candle, hid behind the clothes that hung in a corner of the room and waited. At midnight two dainty, naked elves appeared. They sat themselves down at the workbench, took the leather the shoemaker had prepared, and worked so nimbly, with such unbelievable swiftness, that the shoemaker, in his astonishment, could not take his eyes off them. The elves did not stop until everything was completed, then they sprang up and disappeared, and it was still a long time to daylight.

The wife said to her husband, "These tiny men have made us rich. We must show our gratitude. I feel so sorry for them, running around in the cold without clothing. I will make them shirts, vests, coats and pants and knit them stockings, and you make for each of them a tiny pair of shoes."

The husband agreed, and in the evening, when all was ready, they spread out the clothing, and anxious to see how the elves would react, they again hid themselves and waited. Once more the little people came at midnight. When they saw the clothes, they seemed very happy and quickly put them on. Then they began to hop and jump and dance, and so they danced their way out of the door and never came back again.

THE ELVES ASK A SERVANT GIRL TO BE GODMOTHER

A poor servant girl, who was industrious and clean, each day swept the dirt away from in front of the door into a great heap. One day she found a letter on top of the heap, and because she couldn't read, she brought the letter to her master. It was an invitation from the elves to be godmother at the christening of one of their children.

The girl considered the request, and finally, after it was explained to her that it would not do to turn down an invitation from the elves, she accepted.

Three elves arrived and escorted her to a hollow mountain. Everything was small, but indescribably rich and elegant. The new mother lay in a bed of ebony. Whole pearls served as knobs for the bedposts. The bedclothes were made of gold cloth, the cradle of ivory and the baby's bath of gold.

The girl had stood godmother and was ready to leave, but the elves begged her to visit three days longer. She enjoyed her stay, and when the three days were over, the elves stuffed her pockets full of gold and led her home. But when she arrived, it turned out that instead of three days she had spent a whole year in the mountain.

The elves stole a child from its crib and in its place left a blockhead, with staring eyes, that did nothing but eat and drink.

The mother in despair went to a neighbor to ask for advice. The neighbor told her to carry the changeling into the kitchen, place him next to the hearth, and then set water to boil in two eggshells. That would make the changeling laugh, and once he laughed, he would have to return to the place he had come from. The mother did as her neighbor advised, and when she set the eggshells filled with water to boil, the changeling said:

"Now it's told
as the West Wood I'm old
and never till now have I seen cooking in eggshells."

He burst out laughing, and as he laughed, a crowd of elves appeared, bringing the true child with them. They sat him down by the hearth and took their own fellow away.

Rapunzel

Rapunzel

There once lived a husband and wife who, for a long time, had wished for a child but had not had one. At last, the wife became pregnant.

The couple had a lean-to with a small window in it that looked out on the garden of an evil fairy. The garden was filled with a great variety of herbs and flowers, and no one was allowed to enter it.

One day, as the wife stood at the window gazing into the garden, she noticed a lovely bed of rapunzel. She developed an irresistible craving for a taste of this lambs' lettuce, although she knew no one might have any. Soon she began wasting away and was quite miserable.

Her husband grew alarmed and asked her what the matter was.

"Oh," she replied, "if I can't have some of the lambs' lettuce from the garden behind our house, I'll die."

The husband, who loved her very much, thought to himself, "No matter what the cost, I must fetch her some." One evening he climbed over the high wall, quickly grabbed a handful of lambs' lettuce and brought it to his wife. She made a salad of it at once and ate it ravenously. It tasted so good that the following day she craved for it three times as much as on the day before. The husband saw that he would have no peace unless he picked her some more and again climbed over the wall into the garden. There stood the fairy, and he was terrified. She scolded him angrily, because he had dared to enter her garden and had stolen from it. He apologized as best he could, explaining that his wife was pregnant and how dangerous it might be to deny her anything in her condition.

At last the fairy spoke. "I will forgive you and permit you to take as much lambs' lettuce as you wish, providing that when the child your wife now carries is born, it will be given to me."

The husband was so afraid that he promised, and when his wife gave birth to a little girl, the fairy appeared at once, named the child Rapunzel and took her away.

Rapunzel grew into the most beautiful child under the sun. As soon as she reached the age of twelve, the fairy locked her up in a high tower that had neither door nor stairway and only one small window at the very top. When the fairy wanted to visit Rapunzel, she would stand at the foot of the tower and call:

> *"Rapunzel, Rapunzel,*
> *Let down your hair for me."*

Now Rapunzel had magnificent hair, fine as spun gold, and when the fairy called to her, she opened the window, unpinned her hair and, twisting it around the latch, let it fall to the ground so that the fairy could climb up.

One day a king's son passing through the forest came upon the tower. He saw the beautiful Rapunzel standing at the window and heard her singing in such a sweet voice that he fell in love with her. But, since there was no door in the tower and no ladder could reach high enough, he did not know what to do. Still, he returned each day until once he saw the fairy come and heard her say:

> *"Rapunzel, Rapunzel,*
> *Let down your hair."*

Then he saw what ladder was used to get into the tower. He made sure to remember the words spoken by the fairy, and the following day, after dark, he came to the tower and called:

> *"Rapunzel, Rapunzel,*
> *Let down your hair."*

Rapunzel let down her hair, and when it reached the ground, the prince took hold and climbed up.

Rapunzel was frightened at first, but after a short time, she liked the young prince so much that she agreed he might come and visit her every day.

And so they lived for a long time gaily and happily, and the fairy knew nothing about it, until one day Rapunzel said to her, "Madam Gothel, I wonder why my clothes are getting tight. They don't seem to fit me any more."

"You godless child, what must I hear?" the fairy said, for she saw at once that Rapunzel was going to have a baby. In her rage at having been deceived, she took hold of Rapunzel's beautiful hair, wound it several times about her left hand, grabbed a scissors with her right hand and, snip, snip, the hair was gone. Then the fairy banished Rapunzel to a wasteland, where she lived most unhappily and, after a time, gave birth to twins, a boy and a girl.

The evening of the same day that she had sent Rapunzel away, the fairy tied Rapunzel's cut-off hair to the window latch. When the prince came and called:

"*Rapunzel, Rapunzel,*
Let down your hair,"

the fairy let the hair fall.

The prince's astonishment was indeed great when instead of his beloved Rapunzel he saw Madame Gothel.

"Let me tell you, scoundrel," said the infuriated fairy, "your Rapunzel is lost to you forever."

The prince was in such despair that he threw himself from the tower, and though he did not die, he was blinded by his fall. He remained in the forest, stumbling sadly about, living on grasses and herbs, and did nothing but weep.

After a long time he wandered to the wasteland where unhappy Rapunzel lived with her two children. He heard a voice and thought he knew it. At the same moment Rapunzel recognized him. She threw her arms around him and two of her tears fell on his eyes. Slowly everything grew clear, and he could see once again.

About Simpletons

About Simpletons

THE GOLDEN GOOSE

There was once a man who had three sons, the youngest of whom was a simpleton.

One day the eldest son said, "Father, I am going to the forest to cut wood."

"Let it be," said the father, "or you'll come back with a bandaged arm."

But the son paid no attention to what the father had said. "I can take care of myself," he thought. He put a tart in his pocket and went to the forest. There he met a little gray old man, who said to him, "How about giving me a piece of the tart you have in your pocket? I'm so hungry."

"Why should I? If I give you any, I won't have enough for myself," replied the clever son. "Be off with you!" He picked up his ax and began to chop down a tree. But he had not been working long before he missed his aim. The ax hit him in the arm, and he had to go home and have the wound bandaged.

Then the second son went to the forest. He, too, met the little man, who asked him for a piece of his tart. He, too, refused and, because of it, hit himself in the leg and had to be carried home.

Finally the simpleton went to the forest and the little man asked him, as he had asked his brothers, for a piece of his tart.

"You may have it all," said the simpleton, and gave it to him.

Then the little man said, "Chop down this tree, and you will find something."

The simpleton chopped away, and when the tree fell, there on the stump sat a golden goose. The simpleton took the goose with him to an inn, where he intended to stay the night. He asked for a single room and put the goose into it. Then he went out. The inn-keeper's three daughters, who had seen the goose, each decided they must have one of its golden feathers.

The eldest daughter said, "I'll go upstairs and if I don't return soon, come after me." She went up to the room, approached the goose, but no sooner had she touched one of its feathers than she stuck to it and could not pull away. As she didn't come down, the second sister went upstairs. The moment she saw the goose, she, too, could not resist the desire to pull out one of its feathers. The eldest did her best to warn her, but the second sister would not listen, and once she touched the goose, she could not let go either. After waiting quite awhile, the third daughter decided to follow her sisters. They warned her, for heaven's sake, to stay away from the goose, but she paid no attention, thinking she must have a feather, and she too stuck fast.

The following morning, the simpleton put the goose under his arm and left the inn, and the three girls were forced to follow after him. On the way, they met the priest.

"For shame, nasty girls, to chase a young fellow so brazenly," he scolded. He took hold of one of them by the hand to pull her away, but his hand stuck in hers, and so he was forced to go along with the others. Soon, they met the sexton.

"Father, where are you rushing to? There's no baptism today," cried the sexton. He ran up to the priest, grabbed him by the sleeve and was forced to join the procession. Now there were five, walking along one after the other. They met two peasants coming from the fields, carrying their hoes. The priest called to them, asking them to help get the marchers separated. But they had hardly touched the sexton when they themselves were joined on. And now there were seven in a row, following the simpleton and the goose.

At last they came to a city ruled by a king who had so serious a daughter that no one could make her laugh. The king had let it be known that whoever could make the princess laugh would have her hand in marriage.

When the simpleton heard about this, he led his procession to the princess. As soon as she saw the parade, she began to laugh and couldn't stop.

But when the simpleton claimed his bride, the king, who was dissatisfied with the match, demurred, saying that before the simpleton could marry the princess, he must find a man who could drink a cellarful of wine.

And so the simpleton went back into the forest, to the spot where he had chopped down the tree. There sat a man with a very troubled expression. The simpleton asked him what was making him unhappy.

"Oh, I'm so thirsty and I can never get enough to drink. I've just finished a keg of wine, but what use is one drop of water on a hot stone?"

"I can help you," the simpleton replied. "Come along with me, and you will be able to quench your thirst."

He led the man to the king's wine cellar. The man squatted before one barrel after another, until his haunches hurt, and drank and drank, and before the day was over he had finished all the wine in the cellar.

The simpleton again claimed his bride, but the king was still annoyed that such a lowly fellow, whom everyone called a simpleton, should have his daughter, and so he made another condition: The simpleton must find him a man who could eat a mountain of bread.

The simpleton again returned to the forest, to the spot where he had chopped down the tree. There sat a man with a sorrowful face. As he tightened his belt, he said, "I've eaten a whole ovenful of hard crusts, but what good does that do? With my great hunger, it's had no effect at all, and I can do nothing but tighten my belt so that I don't die of starvation."

When the simpleton heard these words, he was very happy and said, "Get up and come with me, and you will be able to eat your fill."

He took him to the king, who ordered all the flour in the kingdom to be gathered together and baked into a mountain of bread. The man from the forest stood himself before it and began to eat. At the end of a day and a night the mountain had disappeared.

The simpleton again claimed his bride. Still the king tried to get out of the bargain. He demanded a ship that could travel on land as well as on water. Should the simpleton find such a ship, he could have the princess at once.

The simpleton returned to the forest for the third time. There he found the little gray old man to whom he had given his tart, and the little man said, "I drank and ate for you and now I will also give you the ship, because you were kind to me." Then he gave him a ship that could travel on land and sea, and when the king saw it, he was forced to let the marriage take place. The simpleton became the king's heir and the couple lived contentedly together for many years.

THE WHITE DOVE

A beautiful pear tree grew in front of a king's palace, and each year it bore rich fruit. But as the pears grew ripe, someone stole them away, and no one had been able to discover the thief.

The king had three sons, the youngest of whom was considered a fool and was called Simpleton. The king ordered his eldest son to stand guard beneath the tree every night for a year so that he might discover the thief. The son did as his father requested and, day after day, as it grew dark, stationed himself beneath the tree. The tree blossomed and grew heavy with fruit, and when the pears began to ripen, the prince became more watchful than ever. At last the pears were ripe and were to be picked the following day. But that very night, the prince could not help falling asleep. In the morning the pears were gone, and there was nothing left on the tree but green leaves.

Then the king ordered his second son to guard the tree for the next year, but things went no better for him than for his brother. It happened again that on the night before the pears were to be harvested, the second brother was overcome by sleep and in the morning all the fruit was gone.

At last it was Simpleton's turn, and the king ordered him to keep watch over the tree. All the court laughed at the idea. Simpleton, however, did as he was told and on the last night of his watch managed to remain awake. He saw a white dove fly to the tree, pick off a pear, carry it away and return for the next one. As it flew off with the last pear, Simpleton stood up and tried to follow it. But the dove flew to the top of a high mountain and disappeared into a crevice at the summit. Suddenly Simpleton noticed a little gray man standing nearby.

"God bless you," Simpleton said in greeting.

"God has blessed me this moment through your words," replied the little man. "They have released me from an enchantment. Climb down among those rocks and you will find good fortune."

Simpleton climbed a long way down, and when he reached bottom, he saw the white dove enmeshed in a spider's web. When she caught sight of him, she began to tear her way out of the web, and by the time she had broken through the last bit of web, a beautiful princess stood before him. Simpleton's coming had also broken the spell which had transformed her.

They were married and Simpleton became a rich king and ruled over his land with great wisdom.

THE QUEEN BEE

Two sons of a king went adventuring and fell into such a wild and dissolute way of life that they would not come home again. The king's youngest son, Simpleton, set out to look for his brothers. When he found them, they only laughed at him, asking how he thought he could make his way in the world when they, who were so much cleverer, had failed.

Nevertheless they continued on together. As they rode along, they came upon an ant hill. The older brothers wanted to break it up so that they might amuse themselves by watching the frightened ants scurrying about, trying to carry their eggs to safety. But Simpleton said, "Leave the insects in peace. I won't let you harm them."

And so the three brothers continued on until they came to a lake in which ducks were swimming. The older brothers decided to catch a pair of ducks and roast them to make a meal. But Simpleton said, "Leave the birds in peace. I won't let you harm them."

After a time, the brothers came to a tree with a beehive brimming over with honey. The older brothers were about to make a fire under the tree in order to smoke out the bees and get at the honey. But Simpleton stopped them by saying, "Leave the bees in peace. I won't let you harm them."

The brothers then came to a castle where there was not a living soul to be seen, but where the barns were filled with stone horses. The brothers entered the castle and made their way from room to room until they came to a closed door on which hung three keys. In the middle of the door there was a small window, through which they could look into the room beyond. In the room was a little gray old man, sitting at a table. They called to him once and twice, but he did not seem to hear them. When they called a third time, he stood up and came out. He said not a word, but led them to a richly laden table. When they had finished eating, he showed each one of them to a separate sleeping place.

The following morning, he woke the eldest and led him to a stone tablet on which were inscribed three tasks which, when accomplished, would deliver the castle from its enchantment.

In the forest under the moss lay hidden thousands of pearls belonging to the three princesses of the castle. The first task was to gather them all by sundown. Should even one pearl be missing, he who undertook the task would be turned to stone.

The eldest prince went to the forest but, after searching all day, found only a hundred pearls and so was turned to stone.

The next day, the second brother undertook the search, but like the eldest was turned to stone, because he found only two hundred of the pearls by sundown.

It was Simpleton's turn to search the moss. But it was such difficult and slow work to find the pearls that he sat down on a stone and began to weep. As he sat there crying, the ant ruler whose hill he had saved came along with five thousand ants. It did not take long before they had gathered all the pearls together in a single heap.

The key to the princesses' bedroom lay at the bottom of the castle lake. The second task was to find it. When Simpleton arrived at the lake, the ducks whom he had saved from his brothers swam over to help him. They dove down into the water and brought up the key from its depths.

The third task was the most difficult of all. It was to point out the youngest and sweetest of the king's three sleeping daughters. The princesses looked exactly alike and there was nothing to distinguish one from the other excepting that the eldest had eaten a piece of sugar, the second a bit of syrup and the youngest a spoonful of honey before their enchantment. It was only from their breaths that one might discover which princess had eaten the honey. Now the queen bee whose hive Simpleton had saved came flying in. She tasted the mouth of each sister and settled on the lips of the princess who had eaten the honey. And so Simpleton knew which was the youngest of the three.

The enchantment was immediately broken. All who had been asleep awoke, and those who had been turned to stone returned to life. Simpleton married the youngest and sweetest princess and became king after her father's death. His two brothers had each to be content with one of the elder princesses.

There once was a king who sent his three sons out into the world: Whichever one returned with the finest linen yarn was to be heir to the throne.

And in order that they know which way to go, the king stood in front of the palace and blew three feathers into the air. Each prince, in turn, was to pick a feather and follow it. The eldest brother chose first and decided on the feather that had blown to the west. The second prince was next, and he chose the feather that had drifted eastward. The third feather, however, had landed on a stone close to the palace, and so the youngest prince, Simpleton, had no choice but to remain at home. His brothers laughed at him and suggested that he look for the linen yarn beneath the stone.

Simpleton sat himself down on the stone and wept, and as he sat there sobbing, the stone shifted, revealing a marble slab with a ring in it. Simpleton took hold of the ring and pulled up the slab. Beneath it was a stairway leading underground. He climbed down the stairway until he came to a vaulted chamber where a young girl sat spinning flax. She asked Simpleton why his eyes were so red with weeping. He explained that he must find the finest linen yarn in the world and yet must not go forth to seek it. The girl gave him the yarn she had been spinning, which was as fine as linen yarn can be, and told Simpleton to bring it to his father. When he ascended the stairs again, it turned out that he had been away for a long time and that his brothers had already returned. Each brother believed he had brought the finest yarn back with him, but when they showed what they had found, Simpleton's was the best.

By rights the kingdom should have been his. But the others were dissatisfied and talked the king into setting them still another task.

The king then demanded the most beautiful carpet in the world and again blew three feathers into the air so that each prince would know which direction to take. The third feather fell on the stone once more, and Simpleton had to remain where he was. And as before, the other two brothers each went in a different direction— one east and one west. Simpleton moved the stone and descended the stairway. He found the girl busily weaving a beautiful carpet in bright, burning colors.

When it was finished, she said, "This carpet was woven for you. Take it with you. No one in the world has so beautiful a carpet."

Simpleton took the carpet to his father and again met his brothers, who thought they had brought back the loveliest rugs to be had anywhere. When Simpleton's was chosen, they again complained until the king was forced to set them a third task. This time the son who returned with the most beautiful maiden would be declared the king's heir. The feathers were blown into the air, and for the third time, Simpleton's landed on the nearby stone. He followed the stairway and when he came to the girl, he told her that the king had once again given him a most difficult mission.

But the girl said she would help him and advised him to descend even deeper, and he would find the maiden who was the most beautiful of all.

Simpleton climbed down farther and farther until he came to a room where everything shimmered with gold and precious stones, but in the midst of it all, there sat a nasty frog, who said to him, "Hold me fast and take me under water."

Simpleton did not want to do so, and the frog cried out a second and then a third time.

"Hold me fast and take me under water."

Simpleton could no longer refuse. He took the frog, brought it to a lake and jumped into the water with it. No sooner did the water touch the frog, than Simpleton held the most beautiful maiden in his arms. He brought her to his father and she was a thousand times more beautiful than the maidens brought back by the other princes.

In all fairness, Simpleton had now surely earned the heirship to the kingdom. But his brothers insisted on still another test: The prince whose lady could jump to the height of a ring suspended from the ceiling of the palace hall should be the chosen heir.

And the king agreed to their request.

The lady of the eldest prince could hardly jump half the height. The lady of the second prince came somewhat closer, but Simpleton's lady jumped as high as the ring. At that point all had to agree. The king declared Simpleton his heir, and after his father's death, Simpleton ruled long and wisely.

The Water of Life

The Water of Life

There once was a king who took sick and believed he would never get well again. This grieved his three sons so much that they went down to the castle garden and wept. There an old man saw them and asked why they were so unhappy. They told him that their father was ill and nothing could save him.

But the old man said, "I know a remedy. It is called the water of life. If he drinks it, he will be saved. However, it is very difficult to find."

"I'll find it all right," said the eldest son. He went to the sick king and asked permission to go in search of the water of life, which alone could cure him.

"No," said the king. "I would rather die than let you risk your life on such a dangerous quest."

But the prince persisted until the king gave in. In his heart the prince also thought, "If I bring back the water, the king will love me best and I will inherit the kingdom."

And so he rode forth. When he had ridden for a time, he saw a dwarf standing in the middle of the road.

"Where are you off to in such a hurry?" called the dwarf.

"Never mind, little man," the prince replied haughtily. "It's none of your business," and he rode on. The dwarf was angered and at once cast an evil spell over the prince. Soon afterward, the prince came to a gorge, and the deeper he rode into it, the narrower it got, until he could go no farther. Nor could he turn his horse, nor dismount, but remained imprisoned where he was.

The sick king waited and waited for his son, but the prince did not return home. Then the second prince said, "Father, I will go in search of the water of life," and at the same time he thought, "This is a good idea, for should my brother be dead, the kingdom will be mine."

As before, the king at first refused to let his son go but, in the end, gave in. The prince took the same path as his brother. He, too, met the dwarf, who hailed him and said, "Where to in such a hurry?"

"You gnome," the prince said insolently, "it's none of your business," and rode away. And the dwarf put a curse on the second prince who, like his brother, came to a gorge, and rode into it, until he could go neither backward nor forward. Such is the fate of the arrogant.

When the second prince failed to return, the king's youngest son announced that he would go in search of the water, and this time too, the king at first refused and was finally forced to give his consent. When the youngest prince came to the dwarf and was asked, "Where to in such a hurry?" he replied, "My father is dying and I am going in search of the water of life to save him."

"Do you know where to find it?"

"No," replied the prince.

"Well, I will tell you, because you spoke to me politely," said the dwarf. "It flows from a well in the enchanted castle. Take this iron rod and these two loaves of bread. You will need them. When you come to the castle gate, tap three times and it will open. Inside two lions will be lying in wait with their jaws agape. Throw a loaf of bread to each and they will be subdued. Then you must hurry and fetch the water of life before the clock strikes twelve, or the gate will shut by itself and you will be locked in."

The prince thanked the dwarf, took the rod and the loaves and went to the castle, where everything was as the dwarf had described it. As soon as he had quieted the lions, he made his way through the castle. First he came to a large and beautiful drawing room in which some enchanted princes were sitting about. He removed their rings and also took away with him a sword and a loaf of bread that lay there. Farther inside, he came to the room of a princess. She was overjoyed to see him and kissed him, since his coming had broken the spell that had kept her captive. In reward, her entire kingdom was now to be his. He must return in a year when their wedding would take place. She then directed him to the well which contained the water of life and cautioned him to hurry and fetch it before the clock struck twelve. He continued on through the castle and at last came to a room with a freshly made bed, and because he was so tired, he decided to lie down and rest a bit. But the moment he lay down he fell asleep, and when he awoke, the clock was striking a quarter to twelve. He jumped up quite frightened, rushed to the well, took a beaker that stood nearby, filled it and ran quickly to get away in time. He had no sooner got out of the gate than the clock struck twelve and the gate shut with such force that it nicked off a bit of his heel. The prince, however, was overjoyed to have the water of life and started for home.

On his way, he again met the dwarf. When the dwarf saw the bread and the sword, he said, "These will bring you good fortune, for this sword can conquer whole armies and this loaf can never be eaten up."

Then the prince thought to himself, "I don't want to return home without my brothers." Aloud he said, "Dear dwarf, can you not tell me where my brothers are? They left before I did, to seek the water of life and did not return home."

"They sit imprisoned between two mountains," replied the dwarf. "I cast a spell over them because they were insolent."

The prince implored the dwarf to set his brothers free, and the dwarf in the end relented, but warned the prince saying, "Beware of them. They are evil-hearted."

When the prince saw his brothers arrive, he was overjoyed. He related to them how he had found the water of life and had brought back a beakerful. He also told them about the beautiful princess whom he had freed and to whom he was to return in a year's time,

when their wedding would take place, and a great kingdom would be his.

Together the brothers continued on their way. They came to a land where there was hunger and war, and whose king believed he must perish in need.

The youngest prince went to the king and gave him the loaf of bread. With it the king was able to feed his entire country. Then the prince gave the king his sword, and with it the king conquered the armies of his enemies and was able again to live in peace and quiet.

The youngest prince took back his loaf of bread and his sword, and the three brothers rode on. But they came to two more countries where hunger and war reigned, and each time the youngest prince gave the sovereign the loaf and the sword, and in this way he saved three kingdoms.

Then the brothers embarked on a ship and sailed over the ocean.

During the journey the two elder brothers conferred together. "Our youngest brother found the water of life, and surely our father will give him the kingdom. We will be cheated out of our fortune, though it is rightfully ours by birth," they reasoned.

They became revengeful and agreed upon a plan that would destroy their brother. They waited until he was fast asleep, poured the water of life out of its beaker and replaced it with bitter sea water, taking the water of life for themselves.

When they arrived home, the youngest son brought his beaker to the king so that he could drink the water of life and be cured. But the king had hardly touched the bitter sea water when he became sicker than ever before. As he lay there moaning, the elder sons came in and accused the youngest of wanting to poison their father. They had found the true water of life, they said, and they gave it to the king to drink.

The king tasted it and at once felt his sickness disappearing. Soon he was as strong and healthy as in the days of his youth.

The elder brothers sought out their younger brother and mocked him. "It's true, you found the water of life but though you did the work, we've collected the pay. Why didn't you keep your eyes open? We stole it while you slept on board ship, and when the year is out one of us will go and marry your beautiful princess. Just be sure that you don't betray us to our father. In any case, he won't believe a word you say, but mind, if you talk, you'll lose your life. Keep quiet and your life will be spared."

The old king was indeed angry at his son. He believed the youngest had really wanted to poison him. He called the court together and announced that he had condemned the prince to be secretly shot. Soon after, the prince went hunting, and one of the king's hunters accompanied him. As they rode into the forest, the prince noticed that the hunter looked sad.

"Dear hunter," he asked, "what troubles you?"

"I should not tell you, but I must," the hunter replied.

"Out with it," urged the prince. "Whatever it is, I will forgive you."

"Alas," said the hunter, "I am to shoot you dead on the king's orders."

71

The prince grew frightened and said, "Dear hunter, spare my life and I will give you my princely clothes in exchange for your poor hunter's suit."

"That I will gladly do," the hunter said. "I could not have brought myself to kill you."

They exchanged clothing, and the prince continued on his way through the forest alone.

After a time, three wagons, full of gifts, gold and precious stones, arrived at the court for the youngest prince. They had been sent by the three kings to whom the prince had loaned his sword and loaf of bread so that they could defeat their enemies and feed their peoples.

The arrival of the gifts gave the king second thoughts. It occurred to him that perhaps his youngest son had not been guilty after all. He called his retainers together and said, "If only my son were still alive. How I regret that I had him killed."

"In that case, I did the right thing," spoke up the hunter. "I could not shoot him," and he told the king what had taken place.

The king was overjoyed and let it be known in all the lands that he wished his son to return and that he would receive him with favor.

Now the princess had had the road leading to her castle paved with shining gold and had instructed her servants that only he who rode directly on it was her rightful bridegroom and was permitted to enter. Anyone who rode alongside it, however, was the wrong one and was to be turned away.

As the year was almost up, the eldest prince decided to hurry to the princess and present himself as her deliverer. He intended to marry her and claim her kingdom.

And so he rode forth, but when he arrived in the vicinity of the castle and saw the beautiful golden road, he said to himself, "It would be a pity to ride on such a road." He guided his horse to the right and trotted along next to the road. When he arrived at the castle gate, the guards told him he was not the right one and turned him away. Soon after, the second prince came to the castle. When his horse was about to set foot on the golden road, he thought, "It would be too bad to leave footprints on such a road." He signaled his horse to the left of it and continued on. When he got to the gates, the guards turned him back, saying he was not the right one either.

When the year was finally up, the youngest prince decided to leave the forest, seek out his beloved and forget his sufferings at her side. As he rode along, he thought only of her, wishing that he were already with her, and did not even notice the golden road. He rode his horse directly over it, and when he came to the gate, it was flung wide open, and the princess greeted him with joy. She proclaimed him her deliverer and ruler of her kingdom. The wedding was celebrated amidst rejoicing, and when it was over, the princess told him that his father had sent for him and had forgiven him.

He rode back to the king and told him everything: how his brothers had betrayed him and how he had kept his silence. The old king wished to punish his elder sons, but they had sailed away on a ship, and never again returned home.

Rumpelstiltskin

Rumpelstiltskin

There once was a miller, who was poor but had a beautiful daughter. It happened, by chance, that he was able to speak to the king, to whom he said, "I have a daughter, who knows how to turn straw into gold."

The king immediately sent for the miller's daughter and ordered her to turn a whole roomful of straw into gold in one night. If she failed, she was to die. The girl was locked into the room with the straw, where she sat and wept, for she hadn't the vaguest idea of how to make gold of straw.

Suddenly a little man appeared before her and said, "What will you give me if I turn all this straw into gold?"

The girl took off her necklace and gave it to the little man. He did as he had promised, and in the morning the king found the room full of gold. But the sight of the gold only made him greedier and he ordered that the miller's daughter be put in an even larger room, filled with straw that she must turn into gold.

The little man came again, and she took off her ring and gave it to him, and all the straw was again transformed into gold.

Now, for the third night, the king ordered that she be locked up, this time in a room even larger than the others and heaped to the ceiling with straw. "And," said the king, "if you succeed again, I will make you my wife."

The little man appeared for the third time, but now he said, "I will transform the straw once more, but you must promise that when your first child is born, you will give it to me."

In her great need, the girl promised. When the king saw that the straw in the largest room had also become gold, he married the miller's beautiful daughter.

In due course, the queen bore a child and the little man appeared to claim the promise. The queen offered him everything she could think of and a fortune as well, if only he would let her keep her child. But all her pleading was useless.

At last, the little man said, "In three days I will come to take the child. If, however, when I return you know my name, I will let you keep it."

For two days, the queen thought and thought and thought, and could not imagine what the little man's name might be. She could hit upon nothing and was in despair. On the third day, however, the king, who had just returned from a hunting trip, said to her, "The day before yesterday, while I was hunting deep in the dark forest, I came upon a tiny house, and in front of it, a ridiculous little man hopped about on one foot crying:

"'Today I bake, tomorrow I brew.
I'll fetch the child when I am through.
I've kept my name from friend and foe,
"Rumpelstiltskin" the queen won't know.'"

When the queen heard these words, she was overjoyed.

That same day the treacherous little man appeared and asked, "Lady Queen, what is my name?"

"Is it Conrad?"

"No."

"Is it Heinrich?"

"No."

"Is it, perhaps, Rumpelstiltskin?"

"The devil must have told you," the little man cried. He left in a fury and never came back again.

The Six Swans

The Six Swans

A king, who was hunting in a huge forest, took a wrong turn and lost his way. After a time he came upon a witch and asked her to guide him homeward. She replied that she would not. Only one thing could save him from dying in the forest, she said, and that was to marry her daughter.

The king's life was dear to him and, not wanting to lose it, he agreed. The witch brought the girl to him and, although she was young and beautiful, whenever he looked at her he felt only fear and foreboding. Nevertheless he decided to keep his word. The old witch set them on the right path, and the king and the witch's daughter returned to his palace and were married.

The king had seven children, six boys and a girl, by a former marriage, and because he thought their stepmother might do the children harm, he took them away to a castle that stood in the depths of a forest. It was so well hidden that no one knew how to get to it. The king himself would not have been able to find it if a wise woman had not given him a ball of twine which unraveled itself before him to show the way.

The king loved his children and often went to see them. Soon the queen became curious to know why the king spent so much time alone in the forest. She questioned the servants until they betrayed his secret.

The first thing the queen did was to obtain the ball of twine through a cunning ruse. Then taking along some small shirts, she went to the forest, threw the ball of twine before her to indicate the way and followed behind it. When, from a distance, the six small princes saw someone coming, they believed it was their father and were overjoyed. They ran out to greet their visitor, and the queen immediately threw a shirt over each of them. The moment the shirts touched their skins, the boys were turned into swans, rose into the air and flew away. The queen thought she had got rid of all her stepchildren and returned home. In this way, the girl, who had remained in her room, was saved.

On the following day, when the king came to the forest castle, the girl told him what had happened to her brothers. She even showed him some of their feathers that she had found in the courtyard. The king was horrified, but did not suspect that his wife was responsible for this terrible deed. Afraid that the princess, too, might be stolen from him, he decided to take her home. The girl, who was frightened of her stepmother, although she did not know her, begged the king to let her remain in the castle one night longer and, when it grew dark, ran away into the forest.

She walked all day, and not until evening did she come at last to a gamekeeper's hut. Inside she found a room with six small beds in it. Because she was tired, she hid beneath one, intending to sleep there. At sundown, however, six swans flew in through the window and settled on the floor. They began blowing at one another, and as a cloth is lifted, so were their feathers stripped away, and her brothers stood before her. She crawled out from under the bed, and they were both happy and upset to see her.

"You must not remain here," they said. "This hut is a bandits' hideout. They always come here between forays. We are here only for the fifteen minutes each evening during which we may shed our swan-skins and resume our human shapes.

"But there is a way you can free us forever. If, within six years, you can manage to weave each of us a shirt out of aster blossoms, and, from the moment you begin till the time is up, neither speak nor laugh, the spell will be broken. Even one word, and your work will be in vain." As the brothers said the last words, their quarter of an hour was over, and they were turned into swans again.

The next morning the girl picked the asters she needed, climbed up into a high tree and set about making the shirts. She spoke no word, nor did she smile, but worked diligently. It happened that the hunters of the king who owned the forest came upon the tree in which the girl sat. They called to her to come down, but since she must not speak, she thought she might satisfy them with a gift, and so threw her golden necklace down to them. Yet the hunters still insisted that she climb down. She removed her belt, and let it fall.

When this too failed to appease them, she dropped her garters. Finally she was left with nothing on but a shirt. When they saw she would not come down, one of them climbed the tree and forcefully carried her to the ground. They brought her before their king, who was astounded at her beauty. He wrapped his cloak about her, sat her before him on his horse and took her to his castle. Although she was dumb, he loved her with all his heart and made her his wife.

But the king's mother was enraged by the match and spoke evil of the young queen. The wench was unworthy of the king, she said. No one even knew where she had come from. And when the young queen gave birth to a son, her mother-in-law stole the baby away. She painted the queen's lips with blood and told the king that his wife was a sorceress and had eaten her own child. But the king's love for his wife was great and he refused to believe it. When a second prince was born, the godless mother-in-law used the same deception and again accused the queen before the king. Because the young queen could not defend herself, but only sat speechless, making her brothers' shirts, nothing could save her, and she was condemned to die by burning.

The day the verdict was to be carried out happened to fall on the last day of the sixth year, and the young queen had finished all the shirts but for the left sleeve of the last. And when she was led to the funeral pyre, she carried the shirts with her. The fire was about to be lit, when she saw six swans flying toward her. As they descended around her, she threw the shirts into the air and they fell down on the birds. At the touch of a shirt, each swan shed its feathers and the

queen's six brothers stood, living, before her. Only the youngest brother retained a swan's wing instead of his left arm. Now that she had at last freed her brothers and might speak again, the queen told the king how cruelly her mother-in-law had maligned her. The mother-in-law was at once tied to the stake and burned to death. The king, the queen, and her six brothers lived happily in the palace for a long time after.

King Thrushbeard

King Thrushbeard

A king had a daughter who was marvelously beautiful, but she was so proud, haughty and capricious that she not only turned down one suitor after another but made a laughingstock of them as well.

Once the king gave a great banquet to which he invited all the young men he considered suitable candidates for his daughter's hand. They were lined up according to their rank and station: first the kings, then the princes, then the dukes, followed by the counts and the barons, and finally the lesser nobles.

The princess, who was escorted down the row of noblemen, had some fault to find with each of them. Most of all she amused herself over the crooked chin of the good king who stood at the head of the line.

"Why he has a chin like the beak of a thrush," the princess announced.

From then on, everyone called him "Thrushbeard."

When the old king saw that his daughter did nothing but mock the guests, he became so angry that he swore to give her in marriage to the first beggar who came to the door.

Soon after, a passing minstrel stopped to sing beneath the princess's window. The king ordered the minstrel brought to him, and dirty as the beggar was, the princess was forced to accept him as her bridegroom. A priest was sent for at once, and the wedding took place. As soon as the ceremony was over, the king said to his daughter, "It is no longer fitting that you live here in the palace. Now you must go with your husband."

And so the beggar and the king's daughter left the palace together. On their way they passed through a huge forest, and the princess asked, "Whose beautiful forest is this?"

> "*King Thrushbeard owns the woods you see,*
> *And they might have belonged to thee.*"

The princess replied:

> "*A foolish maid, I was mistaken.*
> *If only Thrushbeard I had taken.*"

Soon after they passed through some meadowland. "Whose lovely meadows are these?"

> "*King Thrushbeard owns the fields you see.*
> *And they might have belonged to thee.*"

Again the princess said:

> "*A foolish maid, I was mistaken.*
> *If only Thrushbeard I had taken.*"

Then they came to a large city. "Whose great city is this?"

"King Thrushbeard owns the town you see,
And it might have belonged to thee."

For the third time, the princess replied:

"A foolish maid, I was mistaken,
If only Thrushbeard I had taken."

By now the beggar had grown quite surly with his wife, who seemed little interested in him and wished only that she had married King Thrushbeard.

Finally they arrived at a tiny house, and the princess said:

"Oh, what a poor, small house I see.
Whose may this stingy hovel be?"

The beggar replied, "This poor, small house is our house, where we will live. Be quick now, start a fire and set the kettle boiling so that you can cook me a meal. I am tired out." But the princess knew nothing about cooking. Her husband had to help with everything and so they managed tolerably well, and when they had eaten, they went to sleep.

In the morning, however, the princess had to get up early and do the housework. Things went badly and after a few days the husband said, "Wife, we can't go on this way any longer, just eating and drinking and not earning any money. You might try weaving baskets." He went out and cut some willows and the princess began to weave them into baskets, but the tough willows soon cut into her hands.

"It is clear you can't make baskets," said the husband, "so you had better try spinning. That will probably go better." The princess sat down and began to spin, but the harsh thread, too, cut her delicate fingers, and they bled.

"You're no good at any work," the husband said very much annoyed. "I'll start a pots-and-pans business, and you will sell them in the market."

At first things went very well. The people were glad to buy pots from so beautiful a vendor. They paid whatever price she asked and some even paid and left the pots behind. When everything was sold, the husband bought up a whole new lot of dishes and again the wife sat herself in the market, hoping to make a good profit. But a drunken hussar rode right in among the dishes and shattered them into thousands of pieces. The wife was frightened and did not dare go home all day. When she finally went home, she found that the minstrel had run away and left her.

For a while she lived all alone in great need, until one day a man came and invited her to a wedding. She hoped to be able to bring back some leftovers that she could live on for a time. Then she put on her cloak and hid a pot and a leather bag, which she had slung over her shoulder, beneath it.

At the wedding, everything was splendid and plentiful. She had filled her pot with soup and her bag with scraps and was preparing to leave. Just then one of the guests insisted that she dance with him. She tried her best to refuse, but he took hold of her arm and swung her into step. The pot fell down and the soup ran all over the floor. The scraps flew out of her bag and scattered. When the guests saw what had happened, they laughed and made fun of her. She was so embarrassed she wished she were a thousand feet underground. She hurried to the door and was about to run down the steps when a man stopped her and brought her back. Glancing up, she recognized King Thrushbeard.

The king said to her, "The minstrel and I are one and the same. I was also the hunter who shattered your dishes in the marketplace. All that happened was intended to teach you a lesson and was your punishment for having mocked me. But now the time has come to celebrate our wedding."

The old king, her father, and his entire court arrived for the festivities. The princess was dressed in magnificent clothing as befitted her station, and a great feast was held in honor of her wedding to King Thrushbeard.

Hansel and Gretel

Hansel and Gretel

At the edge of a large forest, there lived a poor woodcutter. He was barely able to provide daily bread for his wife and two children, Hansel and Gretel. There came a time when he did not even know where the bread would come from, and he had no one to turn to in his need.

One night as he tossed restlessly in his bed, his wife said to him, "Listen, Husband, tomorrow morning, give each of the children a piece of bread, and take them deep into the forest, where it is thickest. Then build them a fire and leave them there. We can no longer feed them."

"No, Wife," said the husband. "I cannot do that. I cannot leave my own dear children alone in the forest. The wild animals would soon tear them apart."

"But if you don't do so," said the wife, "all of us will die of hunger." And she would not let him rest until he had agreed.

The two children, who had not been able to fall asleep because of their hunger, heard what their mother said. Gretel thought there was no hope for them, and began to cry pitifully, but Hansel said, "Be still, Gretel, and don't grieve. I know what to do." He got up, put on his coat, unlatched the lower door and stole outside. There were white pebbles on the ground, and in the light of the full moon, they gleamed as brightly as coins. Hansel bent down and filled his coat pockets with as many pebbles as they would hold. Then he returned to the house. "Don't worry, Gretel," he said, "just go to sleep." And he, too, got back into bed and went to sleep.

Early the next morning, even before the sun had risen, the mother woke them.

"Get up, children," she said. "We're going to the forest. Here's a bit of bread for each of you, but be prudent and save it for your midday meal." Because Hansel's pockets were filled with pebbles, Gretel stored the bread in her apron, and they started off into the forest. As they walked along, Hansel would stop frequently to look back. After a while, the father asked, "Why do you keep looking back and lagging behind? Pay attention and march forward."

"But, father, my white kitten is sitting on the roof of our house and wants to say goodbye to me."

"Fool," said the mother, "that's not your kitten. It's the morning sun shining on the chimney."

Hansel had not been looking back at his kitten. Each time he stopped, he had taken one of the shiny pebbles out of his pocket and dropped it on the path. When they had come a long way into the forest the father said, "Gather wood, children, and I will build a fire to warm us." Hansel and Gretel had soon collected a large pile of brushwood. The fire was lit, and when it had blazed up, the mother said, "Now, children, lie down by the fire and take a nap while we go farther on to find good wood for cutting. When we are finished, we will return for you."

Hansel and Gretel sat around the fire till midday, then they each ate their bit of bread. They waited till evening, but neither their father nor mother nor anyone else came to get them. When it grew dark, Gretel began to cry, but Hansel said, "Just wait a little bit longer until the moon rises." When the moon appeared, Hansel took Gretel by the hand, and they followed the pebbles that shone like newly minted coins and showed them the way.

They walked all night and by morning had arrived home. Their father was truly happy to see his children again. But the mother was secretly very angry and only pretended to be happy.

Not long afterward, there was once more very little bread in the house and at night Hansel and Gretel heard the mother say, "The children found their way back once, and I let them stay, but again there is only half a loaf of bread left. Tomorrow you must take them even farther into the forest so that they will not be able to find their way back. There is no other help for us."

The husband, who would have preferred to share his last bite with his children, was very unhappy but, having given in once before, was forced to agree again. The children had overheard their parents, and Hansel got up in order to go out and gather pebbles, but when he tried to open the door, he found that his mother had locked it. Nevertheless, he consoled Gretel, saying, "Go to sleep, Gretel. The dear Lord will find a way to help us."

Early the next morning, they received their portion of bread and this time it was even smaller than before. As they walked along, Hansel crumbled his in his pocket, and stopping often, he dropped bits of bread along the path.

"Why do you always stop and look back?" asked his father. "Move along now."

"I look back at my pigeon, who sits on the roof and wants to say goodbye to me."

"Fool," said the mother. "That's not a pigeon, it's the morning sun shining on the chimney." Nevertheless, Hansel managed to crumble up all of his bread and drop it bit by bit on the path behind him.

Their parents led them deeper into the forest than they had ever been before. Again a fire was built, and they were told to rest until evening, when their parents would return for them. At midday Gretel shared her bread with Hansel since he had scattered his along the way. Noon passed and evening came and went, but no one came for the poor children.

Hansel comforted Gretel, saying, "Wait until the moon rises, then I will be able to see the bits of bread I strewed along the path, and they will show us the way home."

The moon rose, but when Hansel went to look for the bread, there was none to be seen. The many birds in the forest had eaten it up. Hansel thought he could find his way home in any case and pulled

Gretel along after him, but they were soon lost in the great forest. They walked all night and the following day and were so tired that they lay down and fell asleep. All the next day, they wandered again, but they could not find their way out of the forest. They had nothing to eat, excepting a few berries they found on the ground, and were starving.

At noon on the third day, they came to a tiny house made of bread. Its roof was made of cake, and it had windows of transparent sugar.

"We can sit down here and eat our fill," said Hansel. "I'll have some of the roof, and you try a window, Gretel. It will be nice and sweet."

Hansel had already eaten a good piece of roof, and Gretel had eaten a pair of round windowpanes and had just broken out another, when they heard a sly voice calling from within the house.

"Nibble, nibble, nibble, crunch.
Who nibbles at my house for lunch?"

Hansel and Gretel were so startled they dropped what they had in their hands. At the same moment a small lady, as old as the hills, appeared in the doorway. She shook her head, saying, "Oh, you dear children, where have you dropped from? Come inside with me and you'll be well taken care of." She took each of them by a hand and led them into her house. She served them good food, pancakes with sugar, and apples, and nuts. Then she made up two lovely little beds. Hansel and Gretel got into them and thought they were in heaven.

But the old lady was a wicked witch who ensnared children. She had built her house of bread to trap them, and whenever a child fell into her clutches, she killed it, cooked it and ate it, and those were her feast days. She was happy indeed that Hansel and Gretel had come her way. Very early the following morning, before they were even awake, she got up and went to their beds. "What a tasty snack they will make for me," she thought to herself as she watched the sleeping children.

She took hold of Hansel, carried him to the barn and locked him into a stall. When he awoke he found himself surrounded by wire like a chicken in a coop. There was so little room, he could take no more than a few steps.

The old woman then shook Gretel to wake her and called, "Get up, Lazybones. Fetch water and go into the kitchen and cook something good to eat. Your brother is locked in a stall. I intend to fatten him up, and when he's fat enough, I shall eat him. Now you must keep him well fed."

Gretel was terrified and began to cry, but she was forced to obey the witch. The best food was cooked for Hansel, but Gretel got only crayfish shells.

Each day the old witch came to Hansel's cage and said, "Stick your finger out so that I can feel it and see if you are fat enough."

But instead of his finger, Hansel always stuck out a small bone, and the witch couldn't understand why he stayed so thin.

One evening, after four weeks had gone by, she said to Gretel, "Hurry and fetch some water. Whether your brother is fat or not, I

will slaughter him and boil him tomorrow. Meanwhile I'll fix some dough, and we'll do some baking as well."

With a heavy heart, Gretel brought the water in which Hansel was to be cooked. Early the next morning she was forced to make the fire and hang the kettle, filled with water, over it.

"Tend it till the water boils," said the witch. "I will make a fire in the oven and put the bread in to bake."

Gretel stood in the kitchen and wept. "If only the wild animals in the forest had eaten us, we would at least have died together," she thought to herself. "We would not now be suffering like this, and I would not have to boil water to cook my dear brother in. Dear God, help us in our need."

Just then the old witch called, "Gretel, come to the oven at once." When Gretel came to her, she said, "Look inside and see if the bread is baked nicely brown. My eyes are weak and I cannot see so far, and if you can't either, sit down on this board and I'll shove you inside so that you can have a look around."

Once she had Gretel in the oven, the witch intended to close the door and roast her so that she could eat her too. That is what the wicked witch had planned, but Gretel guessed what she was up to and said, "I don't know what you want me to do. Show me first. You sit down on the board, and I will push you in."

The old witch sat herself on the board. She was light and Gretel shoved her as far in as she could. Then quickly she closed the door and slid its iron bolt in place. The witch, in the oven, began to scream and wail, but Gretel ran off and the witch burned miserably to death.

Gretel had hurried to Hansel and opened his stall. He rushed out and they kissed each other happily.

The witch's house was filled with pearls and precious stones. The children stuffed their pockets, left the house and found their way home.

Their father was overjoyed to see them again. He had not had a single happy day since he had left them in the forest, and now his children were home and he was a rich man as well. The mother, however, was dead.

The Bremen Town Musicians

The Bremen Town Musicians

A donkey had for years faithfully carried his master's sacks of wheat to the mill for grinding. But the donkey was losing his strength and was able to work less and less. His owner had about decided the animal was no longer worth his keep when the donkey, realizing that no kind wind was blowing in his direction, ran away. He took the road to Bremen. Once there, he thought, he would become a town musician. After traveling awhile, he came upon a hunting dog lying by the roadside. The dog lay there panting and exhausted as if he had run a great distance.

"What makes you pant so, Catcher?" asked the donkey.

"Oh," said the dog, "I am old and getting weaker each day, and because I can no longer serve my master in the hunt, he wanted to beat me to death, so I've run away. But I don't know how I'm going to earn my bread."

"I'll tell you what to do," replied the donkey. "I'm on my way to Bremen to become a town musician. Come along and you can get a job too. I'll play the lute and you can try the kettle drums."

The dog was delighted and they continued on together. It was not long before they met a cat on the road who looked as mournful as three days of steady rain.

"What crossed your path, Old Whiskerwasher?" inquired the donkey.

"How can I be happy when I've had it up to my ears? I'm getting on in years and my teeth have gone dull. I'd rather sit behind the stove and dream than chase mice and so my mistress wanted to drown me. Well, I managed to get away, but good rat is expensive, and where shall I go?"

"Come with us to Bremen. You know all about night music and you, too, can get a job as a town musician."

The cat thought this a good idea and joined them.

The three fugitives soon came to a farm, where they saw a cock sitting on a gatepost screaming away at the top of his lungs.

"You'll burst our eardrums," the donkey said to the cock. "What's the matter?"

"Here I promised good weather for the holy day because it is the day Our Dear Lady washed the Christ child's shirts and wanted them to dry. But my mistress has no pity on me. Tomorrow is Sunday and guests are coming, and she has told the cook that she wants me in the soup. I'm to have my head chopped off this very evening. That's why I'm screaming as loud and as long as I still can."

"Nonsense," said the donkey. "Come with us. We're off to

Bremen. You can find something better to do anywhere than die. You have a good voice, and with your help, if we all make music together, it will surely have style."

The cock agreed to this proposal and the four continued on their way.

Bremen was too far to reach in one day. By evening they had arrived at a forest and decided to spend the night there. The donkey and the dog lay down beneath a huge tree. The cat and the cock, however, made for the branches—the cock flying all the way to the top, where he felt himself safest. But before he went to sleep, he looked about in all directions, and it seemed to him he saw a light in the distance. He called down to his comrades that there must be a house not too far away.

"In that case," said the donkey, "let's get up and go there. The shelter here is pretty flimsy." And since it occurred to the dog that a few bones and a piece of meat would do him good, they all made their way in the direction of the light, which grew brighter and bigger, until they stood before a well-lighted thieves' hideout.

The donkey, as the tallest, went to the window and peered inside.

"What do you see, Grayhorse?" asked the cock.

"What I see," replied the donkey, "is a table loaded with lovely food and drink. And the thieves are sitting around it, enjoying themselves."

"That would be something for us," said the cock.

"Yes, indeed. If only we were inside," said the donkey.

The animals held a conference on how to get the thieves out of the house, and at last worked out a plan. The donkey was to stand on his hind legs with his forelegs on the window sill. The dog was to jump up on the donkey's back, the cat was to climb up on top of the dog, and last of all, the cock was to fly up and seat himself on the cat's head. When they were in position, the signal was given and they began to make music together: the donkey brayed, the dog howled, the cat meowed, the cock crowed. Then they broke through the window and into the room to the accompaniment of crashing glass.

The thieves jumped for fright at the unbearable noise and, convinced that the animals were ghosts, fled into the forest in terror.

The four comrades sat down at the table. They weren't choosy about leftovers and ate everything in sight as if they hadn't touched food in a month. When they had eaten their fill, they put out the lights and each, according to his nature and convenience, found himself a place to sleep.

The donkey lay down on the dung heap, the dog behind the door, the cat on the hearth near the warm ashes, and the cock settled himself on a rafter. And because they were tired out from their long hike, they soon fell asleep.

When midnight had passed, and the thieves saw from a distance that there were no longer any lights on in the house and that all seemed quiet, their chief said, "We shouldn't have let them scare us out of our wits."

He ordered one of his men to go back to the house and look around. The messenger, finding all quiet, went into the kitchen to get a light. He mistook the cat's glowing eyes for live coals and struck a match on them. This was no joke to the cat, who sprang at his face, spitting and scratching.

The terrified thief tried to get out the back door, but the dog, who lay there, sprang up and bit him in the leg. As he ran by the dung heap in the yard, the donkey landed him a neat blow with his hind legs; the cock on his roost, awakened by the noise, cried kikeriki.

The thief ran as fast as he could to his chief and said, "There is a terrible witch in the house. She attacked me and scratched my face with her long nails. At the door there is a man with a knife and he stuck me in the leg with it. In the yard there's a black monster, who beat me with a club; and on the roof there sat a judge who cried, 'Bring the scoundrels to me.'

"Then I got away."

After that the thieves never dared to come near the house, and the four Bremen town musicians felt themselves so much at home they decided to remain for good.

And this tale's still warm from the telling, for I've just heard it.

About the Brothers Grimm

Jacob Ludwig Carl Grimm and Wilhelm Carl Grimm were both born at Hanau in Hesse-Cassel—Jacob in 1785 and Wilhelm in 1786. Both attended public school in Cassel, and later the university of Marburg, where they studied law. They spent their whole lives together, living under the same roof, even after Wilhelm's marriage. Jacob was the more scientific of the two, while Wilhelm's interests lay predominantly in literature and music. Together they pioneered in the study of German philology and collected the popular tales, the *Kinder- Und Hausmärchen,* that were to make their name a household word throughout the civilized world.

As time went on Jacob concentrated on his studies of German grammar. His book, *Deutsche Grammatik* (German Grammar), propounded Grimm's Law, one of the bases of the science of philology. And after the original edition of the "Household Tales," the work of editing and expanding was almost entirely taken over by Wilhelm.

In 1840 the brothers accepted an invitation from Friedrich Wilhelm IV of Prussia to move to Berlin, where they remained for the rest of their lives. Both received professorships and were elected members of the Academy of Sciences. Wilhelm died in 1859 and Jacob four years later.